for Bill and Phyllis

First published in this edition in Great Britain 1988
Published by Hamish Hamilton Children's Books
The Penguin Group, 27 Wrights Lane, London W8 5TZ
Text and illustrations copyright © 1984 by Eric Carle Corp.
All rights reserved
A CIP catalogue record for this book is available from the
British Library

ISBN 0-241-12532-4

Arranged and produced by Gerstenberg Co-productions, a division
of Gerstenberg Verlag, Hildesheim, Germany

Early one morning the wind blew a spider across the field.
A thin, silky thread trailed from her body.
The spider landed on a fence post near a farmyard . . .

Eric Carle

The Very Busy Spider

Hamish Hamilton
London

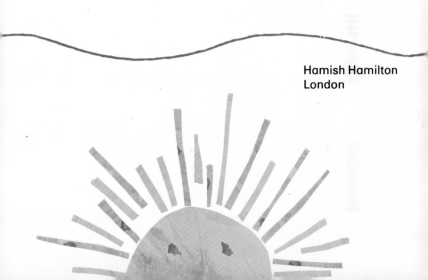

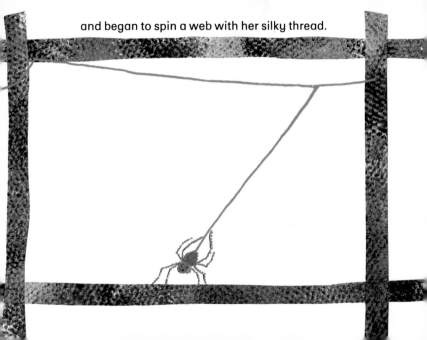

and began to spin a web with her silky thread.

"Neigh! Neigh!" said the horse.
"Want to go for a ride?"

The spider didn't answer.

She was very busy spinning her web.

"Moo! Moo!" said the cow. "Want to eat some grass?"

And the spider caught the fly in her web . . . just like that!

"Baa! Baa!" bleated the sheep. "Want to run in the meadow?"

The spider didn't answer.

She was very busy spinning her web.

"Maa! Maa!" said the goat. "Want to jump on the rocks?"

The spider didn't answer.

She was very busy spinning her web.

"Oink! Oink!" grunted the pig. "Want to roll in the mud?"

The spider didn't answer.

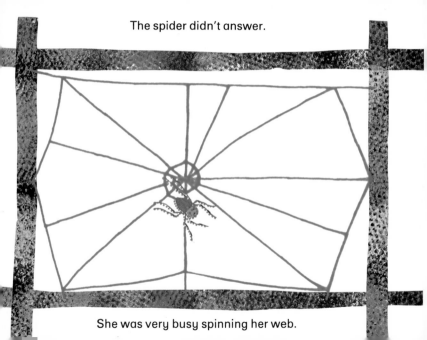

She was very busy spinning her web.

"Woof! Woof!" barked the dog.
"Want to chase a cat?"

The spider didn't answer.

She was very busy spinning her web.

"Meow! Meow!" cried the cat. "Want to take a nap?"

The spider didn't answer.

She was very busy spinning her web.

"Quack! Quack!" called the duck. "Want to go for a swim?"

The spider didn't answer. She had now finished her web.

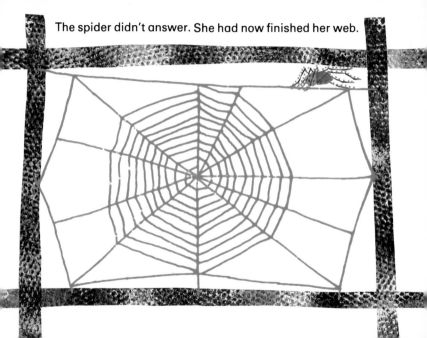

"Cock-a-doodle do!" crowed the rooster. "Want to catch a pesty fly?"

And the spider caught the fly in her web . . . just like that!

"Whoo? Whoo?"
asked the owl.
"Who built this
beautiful web?"
The spider
didn't answer.
She had
fallen asleep.

It had been
a very, very
busy day.

"Whoo? Whoo?"
asked the owl.
"Who built this
beautiful web?"
The spider
didn't answer.
She had
fallen asleep.

It had been
a very, very
busy day.

The spider didn't answer.

She was very busy spinning her web.